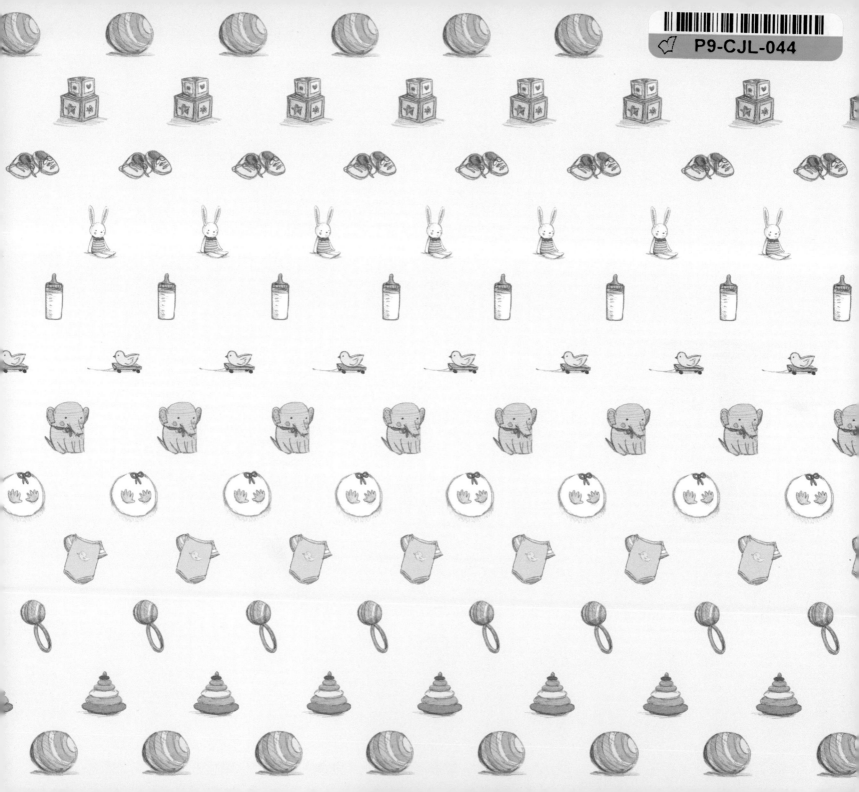

This is for my grandchildren who were first—Sofia, Ella, and Harry.
And for those who came next—Nicholas and Anna —P. M.

For my first sibling, Kristina —S. G.

The illustrations in this book were drawn in graphite pencil on Mohawk paper. They, along with ink washes of patterns and textures, were scanned, assembled, and colored using Adobe Photoshop. The neighborhood and surroundings were inspired by Park Slope in Brooklyn, New York.

This book was edited by Liza Baker and designed by Sasha Illingworth.
The production was supervised by Charlotte Veaney and the production editor was Andy Ball.

You Were the First

By Patricia MacLachlan

Illustrated by Stephanie Graegin

Little, Brown and Company

New York Boston

You were the first....

You were the first to sleep in the basket
with the yellow ribbon wound round.

You were the first to cry.

You were the first to smile.

You were the first to lift your head,

to look at the trees and flowers and sky.

You were the first to laugh at the dog,

that surprising sound coming up from your belly.

You were the first to coo when we sang to you.

You cooed so we would sing again.

So we did.

Over and over and over.

You were the first to lay your
head on our shoulders to sleep.

You were the first to blow a kiss.

You were the first to crawl—

fast, fast, faster down the hallways.

You were the first to walk in your bare feet.
You loved the sand at the beach.

You did not like the grass—

you lifted your feet up so the grass wouldn't tickle.

You were the first to try
to catch the falling leaves,
red and yellow and orange.

You were the first to watch the snow fall—

the first to bundle up in the red snowsuit
and make snow angels.

You were the first to see the bluebirds
come back in the spring—

the first to dig in the garden.

The first to throw a ball—

the first to run from the ocean waves.

You were the first to teach us how to be parents.

One day there may be a second—

or a third—

to sleep in the basket with the
yellow ribbon wound round.

But you will always be the first.